THE STORY OF
MARSH MILL

& OTHER WINDMILLS
IN WYRE

by Ken Emery

All the royalty payments due from the sales of this book
will be going to Wyre Borough Council to help in the
upkeep of Marsh Mill

The Story of Marsh Mill and other windmills in Wyre
by Ken Emery

Copyright© Ken Emery, 1990

Published by Carnegie Publishing, 18 Maynard Street, Preston PR2 2AL.
Printed by T. Snape & Co. Ltd., Bolton's Court, Preston

First edition, April 1990

ISBN 0 948789 52 2

ACKNOWLEDGEMENTS.

I acknowledge the help given to me by Paul Jackson and Alan Alcock of Wyre Borough Council and Ralph Smedley, local historian, all of whom provided me with information about Marsh Mill which I have included in this little book.

Ken Emery.   Dec. 1989.

CONTENTS.

INTRODUCTION.

At long last the future of Marsh Mill is assured. The fact that the mill has survived to this day is most certainly due to concern shown by the local residents for this old building throughout the years and the efforts of many persons, too numerous to mention individually, in preserving it.

Long ago Marsh Mill played an important part in the prosperity of the local community and now history repeats itself with the mill forming the centre-piece of a development designed to attract tourism to the area. With the sails turning it becomes an eye-catching feature of the landscape and the curious are compelled to investigate at close quarters.

This little book is intended to provide those readers with no knowledge of windmills an insight into their development and decline; it tells the story of Marsh Mill and other windmills in Wyre and provides a guide for those visiting the mill.

I have tried to keep the explanations as to the mechanics of the windmill as simple as possible and the diagrams in the book are there to assist in those explanations and are not intended to be serious engineering drawings.

Enjoy your visit to Marsh Mill.

Ken Emery

1

THE DEVELOPMENT OF THE WINDMILL.

Early man knew the nourishing properties of wheat and other cereals and solved the problem of releasing the kernels from their protective outer sheath of bran by pounding the grain between two stones. A more efficient method evolved, that of grinding the corn. The grinding action was achieved by drawing a stone to and fro across a hollow base stone, the saddle quern. They were in use throughout the world and were even depicted in the decorations of the royal tombs of ancient Egypt. The rotary quern was developed and eventually superseded the saddle quern. Grinding action was brought about by rotating one circular stone laid on top of a base stone and fixed by a central pivot. This method produced a continuous grinding action and was soon improved upon using alternative means of motive power — animals, water and wind. From these humble beginnings the windmill was developed together with the unique skills of the miller and the millwright.

The Domesday Book records the existence of over 5,000 mills but it is probable that they were watermills and those driven by oxen or horses. There is a reference to a windmill at Weedley in Yorkshire in 1185 and one, contained in Jocelyn's Chronicle, to a windmill at Bury St. Edmund in 1191.

In medieval times every manor had its mill which provided the lord of the manor with a good source of income as he could compel his tenants to have their corn ground at the manor mill and at no other. This custom was called the milling soke. An old document records the grant of a windmill and soke at Ince near Wigan and the tenants withholding their custom between 1230 and 1283. Eventually the evasion of milling soke by tenants became generally widespread and the custom finally lapsed with the courts showing no enthusiasm to uphold the manorial law. The miller charged for his services by taking a sixteenth of the grain ground, the toll, which he was allowed to sell. This method of payment was very unfair and unpopular as the same toll was demanded at times of poor harvest making it more expensive to grind corn when it was scarce than when it was plentiful. The payment of toll by money became law in 1796.

Early windmills were made of wood and the whole of the structure was pivoted on a fixed vertical post. To bring the mill into wind the miller moved the complete mill by means of a long lever known as the TAIL-POLE. This type of windmill is known as a POST MILL. Later came the SMOCK and the TOWER mills. These mills were more efficient than the post-mills and were static with only their caps and sails being moved into wind. The smock mill is constructed in timber and its tapering tower usually rests on a brick base. Its name is said to come from the resemblance to the smock worn by farmworkers in days long ago. The tower mill, of which the earliest remains date from the 15th century, is built of stone or brick. Marsh Mill is a tower mill. All the three types have survived to this day and working examples exist.

A POST MILL.
MOUNTNESSING MILL. ESSEX.

A SMOCK MILL.
CHAILEY MILL SUSSEX.

The advent of the steam engine heralded the decline of the windmill. Steam driven mills could operate regardless of all extremes of weather and the development of the railway meant that grain and flour could be carried long distances to and from these large and efficient mills. It became increasingly difficult to recruit men who were prepared to work the long and irregular hours necessary for wind-milling and, eventually, many windmills were converted to use alternative power. Local examples are the Pilling Mill installed with a steam engine in 1885 and Preesall Mill now driven by electricity.

The process of roller milling, introduced towards the end of the last century, and the demand for fine white flour, which the windmills could not produce, accelerated the decline. Government regulations, introduced during the First World War, 1914-1918, controlling flour production and the scarcity of bolting cloth at that time, also contributed. Many windmills lapsed into disrepair and were eventually demolished. Many of the sturdy tower mills were gutted and the structure put to other uses. In the Fylde some tower mills have been converted into dwellings, Pilling Mill being one example, and others have survived to be preserved for future generations to marvel at the skill and ingenuity of the mill-wrights. Marsh Mill is such an example, beautifully restored and complete in every detail and now open for inspection by the public.

This magnificent old "wind-machine" is well worth a visit.

THE STORY OF MARSH MILL.

At the time of the construction of the mill there existed an extensive area of open common land known as Thornton Marsh on which the villagers of Thornton grazed their livestock. Even before the passing of the Enclosure Act of 1799 the Government tried to enclose this land but the attempt was thwarted by the lord of the manor, Roger Hesketh. This low-lying land was often flooded when tides were high but in 1799 the lord of the manor, Bold Fleetwood Hesketh, enclosed and drained the marsh which became valuable, fertile farming land. He also built the mill in 1794 the event being recorded by the inscription carved in the stone lintol over the mill door. The mill became known as Marsh Mill and has kept this name up to this day. It was the manorial mill and was probably built as a replacement for the old post mill at Rossall (see page 45). The builder was Ralph Slater who was also responsible for the windmills at Clifton and Pilling. When the drying kiln was built is not known but it was listed in tithe schedules dated 1838.

When Bold Fleetwood Hesketh died in 1819 the estate passed to his younger brother Robert Hesketh, then fifty-five years old, then, on his death in 1824, his fifth son Peter, who was born in 1801, inherited. In 1831 he obtained a royal licence to adopt the name of his maternal forebears and later, in 1838, he became a baronet. Sir Peter Hesketh Fleetwood founded the town of Fleetwood and bankrupted himself in the process and in 1875, after his death, his estate, manorial rights and privileges were purchased by the Fleetwood Estate Company.

The windmill was first operated by a Samuel Thomason, then by his son Richard and later by James Tyler until he sold out in 1896 to Parkinson and Tomlinson - Corn Millers - of Poulton. Around this time the mill was surveyed by Richard Blezzard, Millwright of Preston, who, it is said, was finding it difficult to convince the owner that the sails were rotten and unsafe until one of them obligingly fell off and crashed into the mill-yard in front of them. The mill was modernised in 1896 when Richard Blezzard replaced the original oak windshaft with the present hollow cast-iron one. The sails were replaced with Cubitts Patent Sails, with self adjusting gear, all for the sum of £285-0s-6d. In the old days the miller had the right by law to take any stone or cobble if it was suitable to be used as a bearing within his mill, when the oak windshaft was removed the neck bearing was of a form of red granite. Did a former miller of Marsh Mill exercise this ancient right? The oak windshaft was sold to a company which had been formed to make souvenirs from the timbers of Lord Nelson's old flagship, the Foudroyant, which had been wrecked off Blackpool, close to the North Pier.

Richard Blezzard was the millwright employed by Parkinson and Tomlinson for many years. It is recorded that, in May 1907, he visited the mill to meet the assurance assessor in order to examine damage caused by lightening,

9

his fee for this and making out a report was 15ˢ - 0ᵈ

Edmund Freeborn was the miller employed by the owners in 1896 and he was helped by his sons, Robert and William. They were followed by Thomas Haythornthwaite who also assisted the miller of Staining Mill, a Mᴿ. Armstrong, from time to time.

THORNTON VILLAGE circa 1900.

George Bunn, a native of Poulton, was the last commercial miller having accepted the job on being demobbed after the First World War in 1919. He stayed three years until the mill ceased to operate in 1922 although, by this time, only animal feed was ground.

The mill remained idle until, in 1928, it was used

as a café with the ground and first floors being converted. In 1935 support posts on these floors were removed in order to create more room and this resulted in the second and third floors sagging 4" at the centre causing the mill machinery to come out of alignment and jam. On the 27th May, 1930, a tragedy occurred when two ladies, one of whom had come to inspect the mill with a view to buying it, stepped out onto the fantail platform. The timber was rotten and the platform collapsed. Both ladies fell 75' onto the roof of the drying kiln, in spite of a desperate attempt to rescue one of them, and were killed. One died instantly and the other died later in hospital

COAT OF ARMS
THORNTON CLEVELEYS U.D.C.

The mill was then used as a furniture store and later by a dental manufacturer, the kiln-house now having been converted into a private dwelling. In 1944 the owner proposed to hand the mill over to the National Trust in memory of his son who had been killed in the Second World War but nothing came of this plan.

In October 1954 Marsh Mill was put up for auction but was withdrawn when only one bid of £2,250 was received. There was public pressure on the

Thornton Cleveleys Urban District Council to step in, buy the mill, and preserve it. Finally the mill and the house were purchased by the Council in 1957 for £1,200 with an additional £750 being spent on repairs and renovations with a view to opening the mill to the public as a historical attraction. The project received a set-back when, in December 1962, two of the sails were blown off. However, a restoration fund was launched in November 1963 with the mill becoming increasingly unsafe. A 5ft high scale model of the mill was built by three 3rd year students of the Manchester University School of Architecture and put on public display in January 1964. (This beautiful model can be seen in the Marsh Mill museum.) During the same month another sail was blown off and the remaining one was removed for safety reasons. At a public meeting held in February concern was expressed about the rapidly deteriorating condition of the mill and, following this meeting, the Council agreed to undertake restoration work. This started in August 1965 and the millwrights were R. Thompson and son of Alford, Lincolnshire. The work included reefing stage repairs, the fitting of four new common sails and a new skeleton fantail all at a cost of just over £3,000.

A local man, Walter Heapy, having retired started to work inside the mill restoring the machinery with help being provided from the Council and local engineering firms. He was a founder member of the "Thornton Windmill Preservation Society", formed in 1972 and he continued to work tirelessly until up to his death in 1986.

MARSH MILL AFTER RESTORATION WORK DONE IN 1965.

14

The importance of the work carried out by Walter Heapy, "Mr. Windmill", can not be over-estimated and a plaque in the mill comemorates the appreciation of the public.

On Local Government re-organisation in 1974, the Wyre Borough Council was formed and Marsh Mill had a new

COAT OF ARMS   WYRE BOROUGH COUNCIL.

owner. In June 1977 it was reported that the windmill house was unfit and that repairs to the mill would cost £4,300. By August 1978 the Council was considering converting the house for community use and the mill into a museum. This idea was re-considered in July 1979 when it was decided to demolish the house and re-construct the drying kiln in its former location. The Council also gave consideration to the complete restoration of the mill as a tourist attraction, the use of the lower floors as a museum and the establishing of a craft centre. The drying kiln was rebuilt in 1980 as a Manpower Services Commission Youth Opportunity Scheme, the work being carried out by students from the Blackpool and Fylde Technical College. In September 1983 one sail was blown off and the others were removed by Thompsons of Alford for safety.

By 1986 the ground floor of the mill was being used by the Wyre Guild of Arts and Crafts and, at this time, the Council resolved that a full investigation be undertaken as to the structural condition of the windmill before the sails were replaced. They commissioned L and R Leisure Consultants to prepare a tourism strategy for the Wyre district which would include an investigation into the tourism potential of Marsh Mill. The consultants recommended that, for the mill to have any tourism attraction, it should be restored to full working order with the sails turning regularly thus being a powerful and eye-catching landmark. They also, unfortunately, advocated "the replacement of the rather uninspiring name of Marsh Mill with its connotations of boggy places with the name Wyre Mill to help to establish the Borough's tourism identity." This proposal raised the blood-pressure of most of the locals, including myself, but common sense prevailed, as it usually does, with the Council agreeing the name of Marsh Mill-in-Wyre in order to establish the tourism identity and to, hopefully, satisfy the local residents. They were right, everybody was happy with the name.......a brilliant compromise! The Council accepted the consultants' recommendations : the mill was going to work again after a period of some sixty-seven years.

The creation of a craft village alongside the mill on land in the Council's ownership was agreed and private developers were invited to submit schemes in which they would enter into a partnership agreement with the Council. In February 1988 the scheme for the

present development was submitted by Lanceshire Ltd and approved. It involved the building of craft shops, a village inn and some private dwellings grouped round two village squares at an estimated cost of £1,260,680. The architects were

Cowburn, Bers and Co., the contractors J. and G. Seddon Ltd.,
the sole letting agents Robert Pinkus and Co.

The restoration of the windmill was undertaken by
Dorothea, Millwrights of Bristol, at a cost originally
estimated at £126,500 but which increased as the work

progressed. It was found necessary to renew the timbers of the reefing stage and some joists which were discovered to be unsafe. The restoration work commenced in July 1988 with the cap being removed and replaced by a temporary cover. The mill then looked like a giant pepper pot surrounded by scaffolding. It was painted and the new cap and fan staging were in position by May 1989. With the scaffolding removed it began to look more like the old mill again. After a delay caused by strong winds the Cubitt Patent Sails and the fantail were hoisted into place by a large mobile crane in September. A miller, Alan Alcock, was appointed by the Wyre Borough Council and he assisted the millwrights in their work on the mill machinery.

Finally the big moment arrived. At 11-30 on the morning of the sixteenth of January, 1990, the millwright released the brake, closed the shutters and the sails turned under control for the first time in some sixty-odd years. A good point at which to finish this chapter on the story of Marsh Mill.

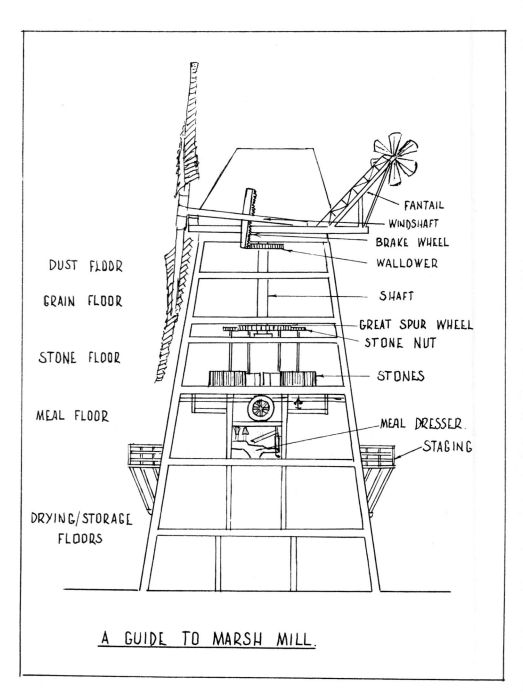

DUST FLOOR

GRAIN FLOOR

STONE FLOOR

MEAL FLOOR

DRYING/STORAGE
FLOORS

FANTAIL

WINDSHAFT

BRAKE WHEEL

WALLOWER

SHAFT

GREAT SPUR WHEEL

STONE NUT

STONES

MEAL DRESSER

STAGING

A GUIDE TO MARSH MILL.

A GUIDE TO MARSH MILL.

STATISTICS.

Base diameter 34'   4th storey diameter 23'
Total height 70'   Length of sails   35'
Reefing stage 26'   above ground level.
Four sets of millstones 5' diameter.

Before we embark on a tour of this impressive tower mill it is necessary to understand how it works, so let us start at the top of the mill on the sixth floor, the DUST FLOOR, where the windpower to drive the machinery is collected by the sails.

THE SAILS.

The sails now in place are of the type known as Cubitts Patent Sails and are similar to those fitted to the mill in the late 1890s. Before that time the common type of sail was in use the frame of which had to be covered with sailcloth to catch the wind. Like a sailing ship they had to be adjusted by increasing or decreasing the area of sailcloth to match wind strength, this is known as REEFING. The problem was that in order to make the sail adjustments the miller had to stop the mill and set each sail, a very inconvenient and time consuming procedure. One improvement was a system invented by a Capt. Hooper, roller reefing, where the area of sailcloth was controlled by rolling it in and out on poles. A significant development was brought about by Andrew Meikle in 1772 who designed a sail which contained shutters coupled with a connecting rod on adjustable springs. The spring tension was set to allow the wind to

21

Hand setting sails

push open the shutters to spill the wind thus preventing the sails
from running out of control in storm conditions. Again the mill had
to be stopped to adjust the springs, but not as often.

Sir William Cubitt in 1807 introduced a refinement to this
system which allowed the sails to be reefed whilst the mill was
operating. This was done by linking the connecting rods on
each sail through a bell crank mechanism to a striking rod.
A hollow windshaft allowed the rod to move against a lever,
at the opposite end of the shaft and then, by means of a
common pivot, to lift a long lever extending out at the rear of
the cap. Some mills used an alternative rack and chain wheel
arrangement instead of the systems of levers used at Marsh Mill.
Here the miller adjusts the shutters by placing on appropriate
weight on a chain attached to the lever. This chain drops to the
balcony outside the third floor of the mill (the REEFING STAGE) so
that the miller can control the entire workings of the
mill from this floor, the MEAL FLOOR.

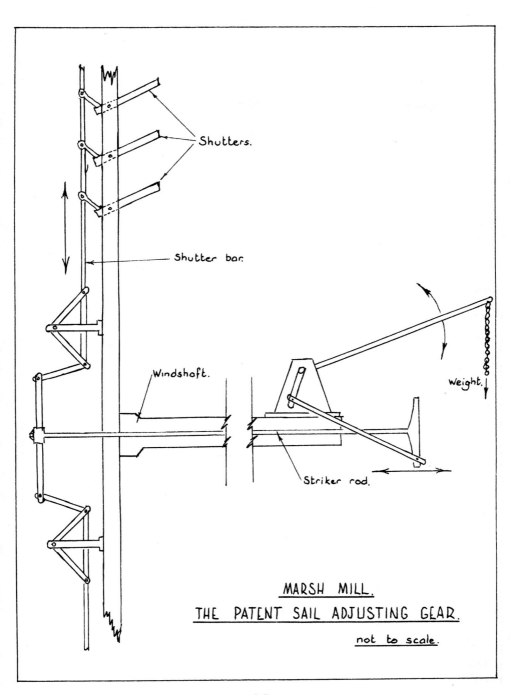

Shutters.

Shutter bar.

Windshaft.

Weight.

Striker rod.

MARSH MILL.

THE PATENT SAIL ADJUSTING GEAR.

not to scale.

THE FANTAIL.

As we saw in the previous chapter the miller had to keep the sails into wind by hand using the tail-pole in the case of the early post mills. The caps of smock and tower mills were moved into wind manually by means of a continuous chain-wheel and worm-screw or, in some cases, by the use of a handcrank. If the miller was slow to reposition the cap into wind during storm conditions the mill would become tail-winded and the cap and sails could be blown off. This was the fate of many windmills.

At Marsh Mill the cap is moved automatically into wind by the fantail, an invention by Edmund Lee made in 1745. It is sometimes known as the Lee's Flier.

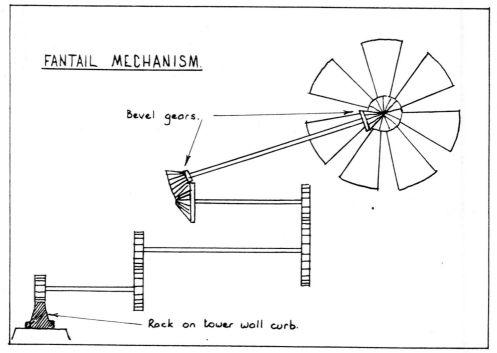

FANTAIL MECHANISM.

Bevel gears.

Rack on tower wall curb.

The wind wheel is mounted on a wooden stage at the rear of the cap and at right angles to the sails. It is turned by the wind, clockwise and anti-clockwise, and drives a system of bevel gears, drive shafts and cogs, to a pinion engaging a rack fastened to the top of the mill tower. When the wheel stops turning, the sails are into wind. It will be noticed that it is sensitive to every change of wind direction and is rarely still. The gear ratio is 1,000 : 1.

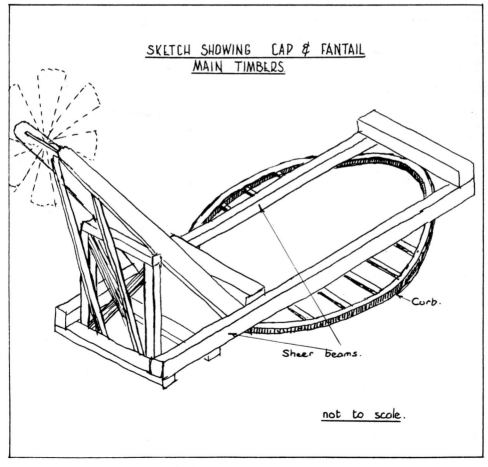

SKETCH SHOWING   CAP & FANTAIL
MAIN TIMBERS

Curb.

Sheer beams.

not to scale.

THE BRAKE WHEEL.

DUST FLOOR— 6th STOREY.

The cap which covers this floor is boat-shaped and clinker built, a feature common to the windmills of the Fylde. The whole is connected to the circular curb made of 4" square section elmwood which, in turn, rests on well-greased cast-iron chairs positioned at intervals around the top of the tower wall. This allows the whole of the cap to revolve and this is known as a dead curb arrangement. Although one of the largest in the U.K. space on the Dust Floor is very limited, much of it being taken up by a heavy suspended oak centering frame. Standing here in the confined space you cannot fail to be impressed by the sheer size of the BRAKE WHEEL, it is 10 ft in diameter and is faced with cast-iron square cogs. These replaced the original hornbeam or apple wood ones when the mill was improved in 1896. The brake wheel is partly surrounded by elm-wood brake shoes connected together and anchored at one end. The other end is fastened to the heavy brake lever which holds the brake on by gravity, and which has to be pulled off by a pulley system when the mill is required to work — a fail-safe arrangement. The brake wheel is made out of oak and beech.

It is thought that the original WINDSHAFT was made out of oak, this being replaced by the hollow cast iron shaft, now in use, in the 1890s. It runs in gun metal bearings and is inclined to facilitate an even distribution of weight on the tower walls and to allow the sails to clear the walls lower down the tower.

The WALLOWER or crown wheel is similar in construction to the brake wheel but smaller having 64 cast iron teeth compared with 80 on the brake wheel. The wallower meshes with the brake wheel at right angles to provide the rotary movement of the vertical shaft to which it is fastened.

GRAIN FLOOR — 5th STOREY.

The eight-sided vertical drive shaft, made of oak and two foot in diameter, passes through the centre of this floor. From this floor, through removable sections, grain of the requisite grade was supplied to the hoppers feeding the stones on the floor below. The miller may have rigged up an alarm bell to ring when the grain in the hopper was running low. They were found in most mills and prevented the stones being starved of grain. This occurrence could result in the stones making contact thereby running the risk of fire from the resultant sparks and the need to redress the blunted stone. The other feature on this floor is the sack hoist windlass which is driven from the STONE FLOOR by a belt and pulley system. When required to be used the belt, which is normally slack thus disengaging the pulley, is tightened by a lever lifting up the end of the windlass. The lever was attached to a rope through a pulley block and by pulling on the rope which passed

through all the lower floors of the mill, the miller could operate the hoist. The windlass chain descends through trap-doors to the ground floor.

STONE FLOOR — 4th STOREY.

On this floor, standing in a half circle against the north wall, there are located the four sets of millstones which grind the grain into flour. The lower bearing of the vertical shaft is supported on an oak beam above which is housed the GREAT SPUR WHEEL which is of similar design and construction to the Brake Wheel and the Wallower. Its diameter is 10'-6" and was originally wholly made of wood. However, cast-iron gearing facing outwards and

bevelled downwards was fitted when the mill was modernised in 1896. It drives the cog wheels - STONE NUTS - which turn the stones and the pulley gear for the sack hoist. The stone nuts are of different sizes so that they turn the stones at the speed appropriate for the various grades of flour produced. They can be individually thrown out of mesh with the great spur wheel by means of the slotted bearings, GLUT BOXES.

The Stones

There are two sets of stones made of French burr from the Marne Valley, sizes 4'-6" and 5'-0" diameter, and two made from millstone grit of 5'-0" and 5'-3" diameter. French burr stones were made up of pieces of stone shaped and matched, cemented together and bound by having an iron band shrunk on round them. The back was made smooth and level with plaster of paris. Each set of stones is enclosed by a wooden casing or TUN. At Marsh Mill the runner stones are driven from above, OVERDRIFT, by steel square sectioned drive shafts known as QUANTS. The runner stone revolves at 125 r.p.m against the lower stone, the bedstone, and both the contact surfaces have identical patterns of furrows cut into them, the furrows running obliquely from the "eye". The grain is repeatedly cut by the scissor action of the furrows which also work the meal towards the outer edge of the stones where it falls out to be collected. It is necessary to redress the stones when the cutting edges became blunt, this can be at

monthly intervals at busy mills. The stone dresser was highly skilled and an itinerant one, on asking for work at a mill, would be asked by the miller to "show his steel", small particles of hardened steel from the mill bill (a stone dressing tool) which became embedded in the skin of the left hand. This was a sure test of the dresser's experience. The windmiller would advertise the fact that they required the services of a stone dresser by setting the bottom sail just in advance of the vertical. It was necessary for the runner stone to rotate in a perfect horizontal plane and this was done by adjusting the iron bridging box which held the thrust bearing. The runner stone was also finely balanced by fixing weights to its upper surface and the bedstone was wedged up until it was perfectly horizontal.

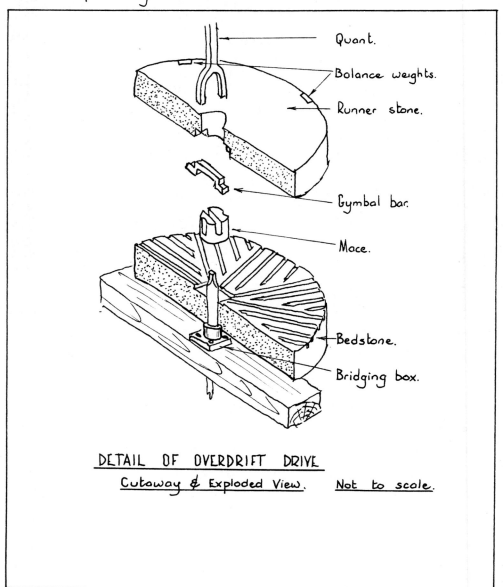

Quant.

Balance weights.

Runner stone.

Gymbal bar.

Mace.

Bedstone.

Bridging box.

DETAIL OF OVERDRIFT DRIVE
Cutaway & Exploded View.   Not to scale.

The Grain Feed.

As previously described, grain is fed from the Grain Floor above into the hopper which is supported over the stones on a wooden frame called the HORSE. The Tun enclosing the stones has an opening over the eye of the stone and into this an inclined tapered chute, the SHOE, fed the grain from the hopper. The quant passes through the eye and, as it turns, the corners of its square section strike the shoe which is held against it by means of a cord and a simple wooden spring. The striking action causes the shoe to vibrate from side to side thereby discharging the grain down the eye in controlled quantities, the faster the quant turns the greater the quantity of grain fed. The miller could also alter the rate of discharge by varying the angle of the shoe by means of a cord, the CROOK STRING, which is fastened to it and is then attached to a TWIST PEG located on the floor below. When ground, the flour spills from the stone edges to the

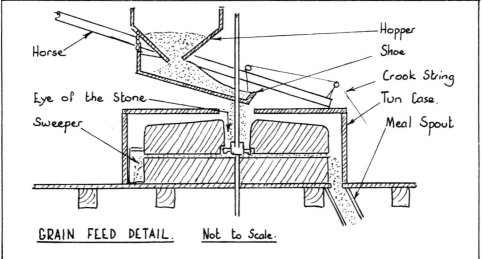

Horse
Hopper
Shoe
Crook String
Eye of the Stone
Tun Case.
Sweeper
Meal Spout

GRAIN FEED DETAIL.   Not to Scale.

floor of the tun where it is swept round by a leather sweeper to the mouth of the meal spout leading to the floor below.

Tentering

The clearance between the stones is critical and can be set from between 1/16" to 3/32" for the various grades of flour or up to 1/4" for milling animal food. These clearances need running adjustments to allow for the different hardness of the grain and for the increases and decreases in the speed of the runner stone, which occurs despite the automatic reefing of the mill. This adjustment is known as TENTERING. At Marsh Mill only two of the stones, the outer left and the outer right, are equipped with the original tentering gear. The outer left is manually operated whilst the outer right is provided with an automatic device worked by governors and patented by Thomas Mead in 1787. The inner left stone is fitted with a more modern compact cast-iron automatic tentering device working on the same principle whilst the inner right stone provides the drive to the BOLTER machine. This machinery can be seen from the Meal Floor.

MEAL FLOOR — 3rd STOREY

From this floor the miller can control the whole operation of the mill, he can operate the sack hoist and has access to the balcony, the REEFING STAGE, from where he can adjust the sails. In the past this floor also, probably, served as the miller's office. There is a confusing array of machinery to be seen and, unless you are an engineer who specialises in windmills (I'm not), it is difficult to understand. I found that the easiest way is to look up at the ceiling

34

and establish the position of the four sets of stones. The HACKLE SCREWS, which adjust the bridging box to allow the runner stone to rotate in a perfect horizontal plane, can be seen and the tentering gear, manual and automatic, can also be identified. Mead's patent tentering works in the following way. The stone clearances are set before use and when, during operation, the revolutions of the runner stone increase, the weighted balls of the governor move outwards lifting a STEELYARD which lowers a secondary lever, the BRAY. This then lowers the supporting beam, the BRIDGE TREE and consequently, the spindle, the mace head and finally the runner stone

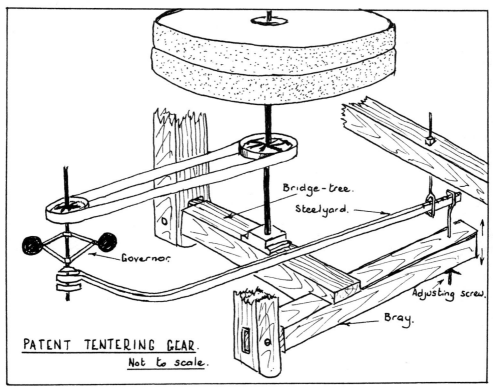

Bridge-tree.

Steelyard.

Governor.

Adjusting screw.

Bray.

PATENT TENTERING GEAR.

Not to scale.

The inner right stone has a horizontal pulley wheel which serves to provide the power to drive the BOLTER machine which is housed in a dust-proof wooden cabinet. The bolter is a framed cylindrical reel, rotating on an inclined axis, which is covered with bolting cloth. Meal is fed in at the top and as the reel revolves wooden bars fixed to it knock against a wooden striker which is attached to the enclosing cabinet. This action forces the flour out through the cloth into the mouth of a chute which goes to the floor below. The bran is fed out at the lower end.

The SIFTER or DRESSER is slung from a frame between

the central support pillars, it consists of a number of
sieves and the sieving action is brought about by the
sifter being mechanically agitated. The speed is regulated
by a governor which lifts and lowers the drive belt on
the tapered pulleys by means of a steelyard. It can be fed
with meal from the outside stone, on the right, by an
auger creeper and a pulley beneath the outer left stone
provides the power to drive the sifter. There are two
elevators on this floor, one for re-cycling the meal
back to the stone floor and one for feeding the sifter.

Two doors open from this floor onto the balcony which encircles the mill, it is called the REEFING STAGE. From here the miller can observe the activities in the mill-yard and, more importantly, adjust the sails.

The carvings in the stone-work of the door openings are interesting but who did them and why? Was it the miller's boy idling away his time or even the miller himself or perhaps the stone dresser as the millstone illustrated shows the correct pattern of furrows? What does the carving of the bird signify? They probably experienced the same problem that exists now, that of doves and ferral pigeons roosting in the cap and in the kiln house roof. This theory is supported by the fact that when they were carrying out the recent restoration work, the millwrights found a mummified carcase of a dove in one of the stone vats.

DRYING AND STORAGE FLOORS – 2ND & 1ST (GROUND LEVEL) STOREYS.

These large rooms were used for storing grain before milling and flour, meal awaiting collection. They now house a museum of milling.

DRYING KILN.

The original drying kiln building was converted into a domestic dwelling which eventually came into the ownership of the former Thornton Cleveleys Urban District Council. In 1981 the Wyre Borough Council took the decision to demolish the house and rebuild the drying kiln, linked to the mill, to recreate the appearance of the mill in its heyday. The details of the building, taken from old photographs, were reproduced during the reconstruction. Care was taken when demolishing the house so as not to disturb the foundations of the original building so that the exact dimensions could be established.

MILL YARD C.1900

KILN HOUSE 1986.

When uncovered parts of the original foundations, constructed of cobble-stones, were found to be sound enough to be incorporated in the new building and can be clearly seen in the firehole area. Like the original the new building is constructed in brick. The accuracy of internal detail was more difficult. However, the task was made easier when the position and shape of the firehole was deduced from the remains found during demolition.

The function of the building is the drying of the grain before it is ground in the mill. The kiln floor was originally covered with specially perforated tiles, supported on "I" section beams, which allowed hot air to pass through the grain spread evenly on the floor. The brickwork of the firebox is vaulted upwards to the kiln floor above and the

41

products of combustion and the drying process are externally vented by means of a louvred cowl on the ridge. The wooden shutters on the kiln floor can also be opened. The dormer in the link has been reconstructed and now extends some 3' from the face of the building with a heavy duty ridge beam to allow the use of a pulley to load the sacks of grain.

THE FIREHOLE WITH THE ORIGINAL FOOTINGS EVIDENT.

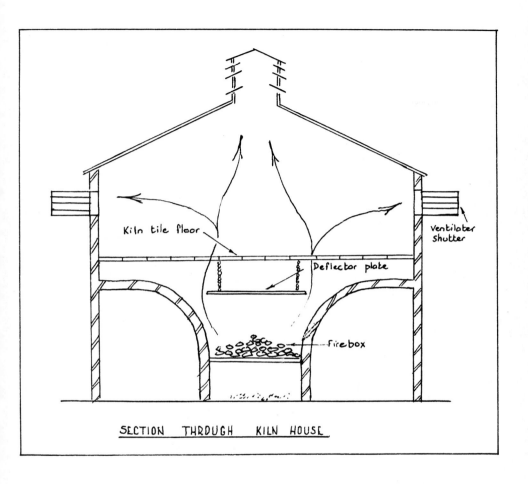

Kiln tile floor

Ventilater shutter

Deflector plate

firebox

SECTION THROUGH KILN HOUSE

The kiln house now forms part of the Marsh Mill museum and contains a commemorative plaque which reads as follows: "This plaque is in recognition of the dedicated work by Mr Walter Heapy (Mr Windmill) towards the preservation and restoration of Marsh Mill, Thornton over a period of 21 years. It also commemorates his being a founder member of the Thornton Windmill Preservation Society formed in 1972 and his close association with its work. 2nd January 1987."

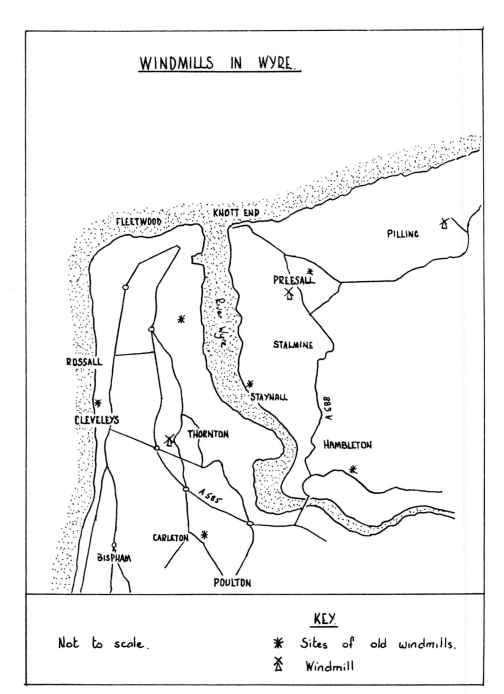

WINDMILLS IN WYRE.

FLEETWOOD

KNOTT END

PILLING

PREESALL

River Wyre

ROSSALL

STALMINE

STAYNALL

A 588

CLEVELEYS

THORNTON

HAMBLETON

A 585

CARLETON

BISPHAM

POULTON

KEY

Not to scale.

✳ Sites of old windmills.
🏚 Windmill

WINDMILLS IN WYRE.

The Wyre district, being part of the flat Fylde plain that was once known as "Windmill Land", has several surviving windmills and there is historical evidence indicating the existence of other windmills which have long since disappeared. Let us now consider these Wyre mills.......... you may be surprised as to their locations and ages.

ROSSALL MILL.

This windmill is shown on William Yates map of 1786 and the symbol used shows it to be a post mill. Its exact location is not known as there are no visible remains, but it is thought to have been situated on the coast just north of Cleveleys but south of Rossall School. When it was built and when it was dismantled is not known but it was most certainly there in August 1702 if we are to believe the account of a shipwreck of the vessel "Employment" in the journal of William Stout of Lancaster. It is related in John Porter's "History of the Fylde", a book first published in 1876.......
"The mate, not being an experienced pilot, was embayed on the coast of Wales but with difficulty got off, and then made for the Isle of Man, and stood for Peel Fouldrey, but missed his course, so that he made Rossall Mill for Walna Mill, and run in that mistake till he was embayed under the Red Banks, below Rossall, so as he could not get off.....this happened on the 8th month 1702........."

NEW MILL.

New Mill is another mill shown on William Yates map of 1786 but this time it is indicated as being a tower mill. Again

45

no trace of it remains so we can only speculate as to its exact position which is thought to be somewhere on land occupied by the I.C.I. near to the Cala Gran Caravan Park.

DICKS MILL.

We know little more about this tower mill which was situated on Poulton Road between Carleton and Poulton. It was known as Dicks Mill and was so badly damaged in a storm that towards the end of its commercial life it was driven by a steam engine. After standing idle for a while it was purchased by a Carleton man who immediately pulled it down and, using the bricks, built the three cottages, 74, 76 and 78, Poulton Road. They can be easily identified by the sandstone plaque on which is carved the likeness of the windmill and the words "Dicks Mill Terrace A.D. 1886".

HAMBLETON MILL.

Again nothing remains of this old wooden post mill which was dismantled at the turn of this century, being then about 200 years old. Luckily it was a popular subject for photographers and artists and, thanks to them, we know exactly what it looked like. It was on the site now occupied by the garage owned by a former Mayor of the Borough of Wyre, Councillor Bob Williamson.

STAYNALL MILL.

This mill was a wooden post mill and is thought to have been in use from about 1500 to 1700. It is referred to in a Commissioner's report before the dissolution of monastries written in the reign of Henry VIII This report listed the sources available to an officiating priest of a chantry at

HAMBLETON MILL 1895.

DICKS MILL

TERRACE A.D. 1880

St. Michaels Church and refers to income from annual rentals and lists "a windmill at Stainall at 12s 8d." Allen Clarke in his book "More Windmill Land" writes about a millstone, probably from this windmill, being built into the pavement of a Staynall farmyard and concludes that the mill's exact location was on the bank of the River Wyre in a field still known as Mill Field.

STALMINE MILL.

Yates's map of Lancashire, 1786, shows a windmill on a site to the west of the A588 and opposite the junction with Old Tom's Lane. The road up the hill past the school to the Seven Stars is still called Mill Lane.

PREESALL MILLS.

Even without its sails and original cap Preesall Mill is still an impressive sight. It stands alongside the road leading into Preesall from the direction of Stalmine and this mill together with Marsh Mill are the tallest in the Fylde. It consists of six storeys and, in its heyday, had sails 38ft long and was encircled with a balcony, the reefing stage. The mill was built in 1839 and replaced an old wooden post mill which stood on the top of Preesall hill, up Mill Lane. This windmill was destroyed in a great storm which occurred in the first week of the year 1839, six months later the construction of the tower mill commenced.

PILLING MILL.

Now converted into a private residence the mill stands in a picturesque setting alongside the Broadfleet at Dam Side. It is said that there was once a water-mill

PREESALL MILL 1989.

PREESALL MILL AS IT WAS

49

PILLING MILL 1989.

PILLING MILL AS IT WAS

50

almost on the same site on which the present mill is built. Ralph Slater, the builder of Marsh Mill, built Pilling Mill in 1808, the work only taking three weeks to complete. Originally it had six storeys with the reefing stage encircling the mill at the second storey. The 63 ft tall brick tower once contained four large sets of stones, one being 6 ft in diameter. There is a local legend about a farm worker agreeing to be tied to a sail as a bet to win a gallon of beer, he managed one revolution before shouting to be released having had enough of the experience. Whether or not he was awarded the prize is not known. The mill's sails and wind cap were removed when it was converted to steam power in the 1880s and the mill continued in use finally closing down in 1926.

BIBLIOGRAPHY

The English Windmill.   Rex Wailes.   1954.

Englands Vanishing Windmills.   A.E.P. Shillingford.   1979.

History of the Fylde of Lancashire   John Porter.   1876.

An Album of Thornton-Cleveleys.   Catherine Rothwell. 1981.

Windmill Land.   Allen Clarke   1916.

More Windmill Land.   Allen Clarke   1917.

THIS delightful handwritten book is the official guide to Marsh Mill in Wyre, the only working windmill in the county, which opened recently in Thornton village. Ken Emery not only tells the story of Marsh Mill up to the present day, he paints a vivid picture of a craft which has now all but died out. Using many exquisite drawings, he guides the reader around the mill, explaining the milling process, the equipment used and the way of life for the millers who made their living in them.

As well as Marsh Mill there are, or used to be, other similar mills on the wind-blown plains of the Wyre and readers will be surprised to learn of their locations and history. For those who have not yet visited Marsh Mill, this book will be a tantalising glimpse into part of Wyre's past and it will encourage many people to go and see the mill itself. For those who have already visited, this book will be a fascinating, informative and attractive souvenir of one of the most interesting and enjoyable working museums in the north of England.

Carnegie Publishing

£1.50 **ISBN 0 948789 52 2**